ACKNOWLEDGMENTS

To be able to reach the world with my thoughts translated into this beautiful story, it wouldn't have been possible without those who add color to my life.

To my friend, Nidhi Podar Mundhra—you were the crayon box ready to fill in my blank drawing. You added a rich and vivid perspective, refining every detail so the book had more depth and personality. Thank you for your unconditional support, your honesty, and above all, your friendship.

To my sisters, Khushboo, Nidhi, and Akriti, for being my extra set of eyes, ears, and minds when I was losing mine.

To Pooja, for carrying my light, for being my light.

To Kishmish, for reminding me to never say never.

To Gillian Barth, for your positivity and ever-smiling attitude.

To my entire family, for being my pot of gold at the end of the rainbow.

To Ivu, for being my Krishna.

To Mom, for dragging me to the bookstore.

To **A**nousha, **A**haana, and **A**ditya, my pick-me-ups
when I'm running out of creative fuel.

You push me (to my fullest).
You pull me (for warm and sometimes smelly hugs).
You piss me off.

I love you, *meri jaans*.

MASCOT KIDS!
an imprint of Amplify Publishing Group

www.mascotbooks.com

You're Truly One of a Kind

©2023 Sonali Patodia. All Rights Reserved. No part of this publication may be reproduced, stored in a retrieval system or transmitted in any form by any means electronic, mechanical, or photocopying, recording or otherwise without the permission of the author.

For more information, please contact
Mascot Kids, an imprint of Amplify Publishing Group
620 Herndon Parkway #320
Herndon, VA 20170
info@mascotbooks.com

Library of Congress Control Number: 2022914280
CPSIA Code: PRKF0323A
ISBN-13: 978-1-63755-544-6

Printed in China

You're Truly One of a Kind

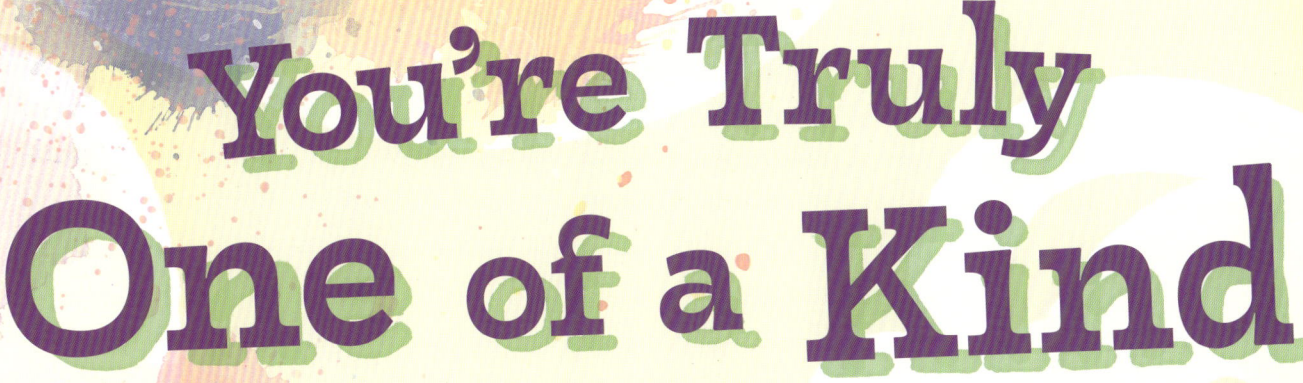

Dear Aiden,
I hope the characters in this book become your friends.
Love,
Sonali

Sonali Patodia

Illustrated by Vanessa Alexandre

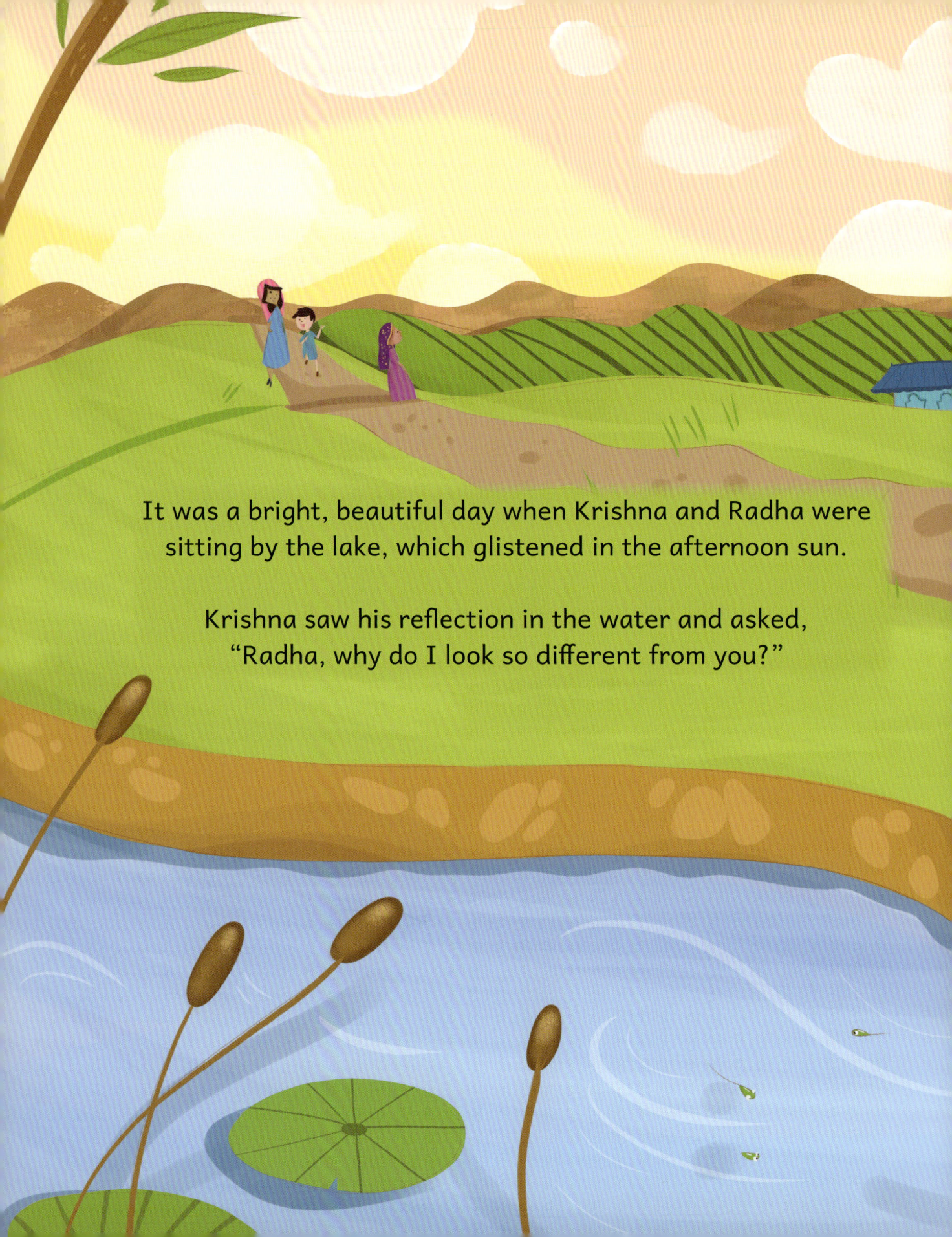

It was a bright, beautiful day when Krishna and Radha were sitting by the lake, which glistened in the afternoon sun.

Krishna saw his reflection in the water and asked, "Radha, why do I look so different from you?"

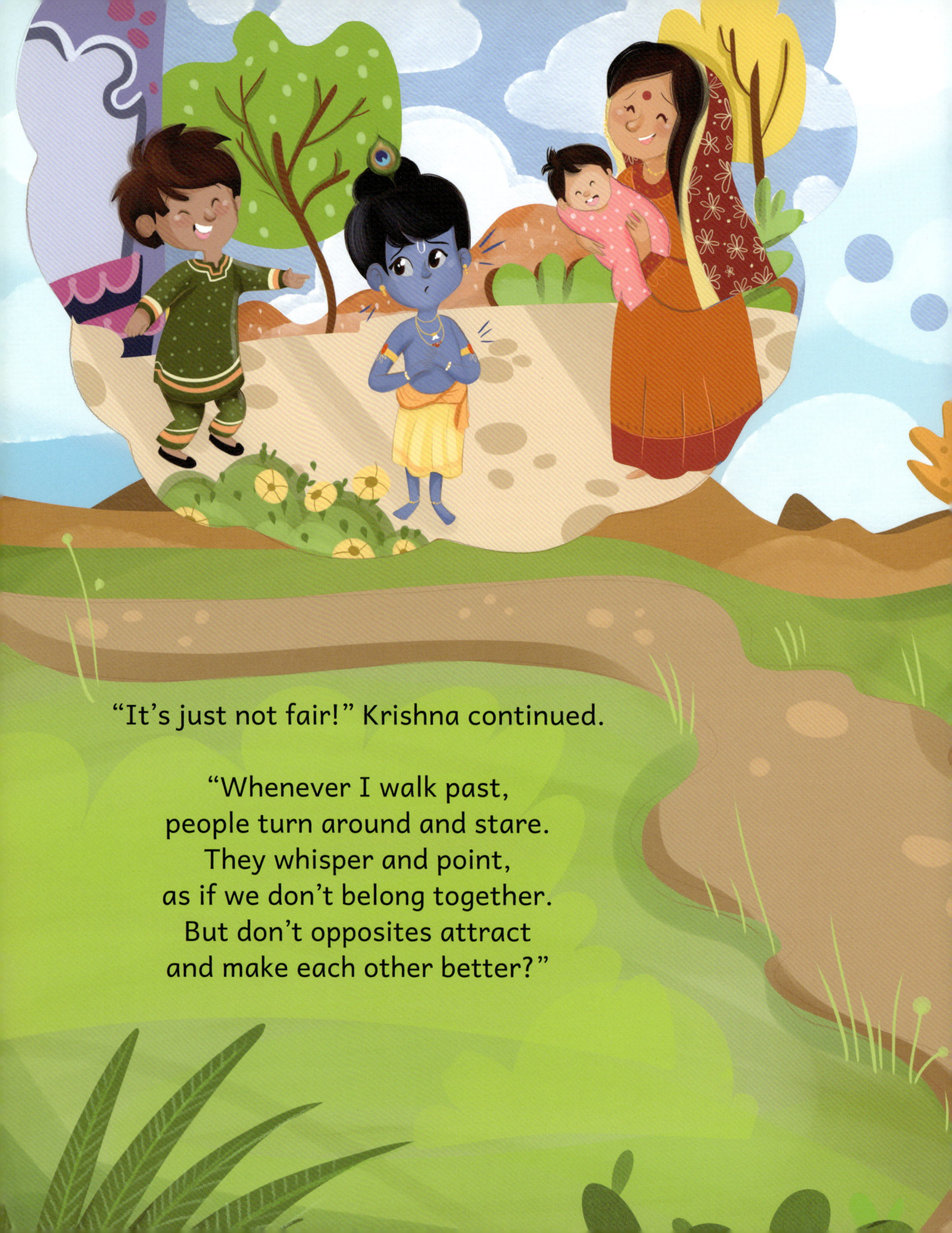

"It's just not fair!" Krishna continued.

"Whenever I walk past,
people turn around and stare.
They whisper and point,
as if we don't belong together.
But don't opposites attract
and make each other better?"

Krishna began walking, lost in deep contemplation.

As Radha quietly went along thinking about what Krishna said, she noticed something.

She said,
"Krishna, look at this family.
Each member is so different.
One has long hair, the other is bald.
One is towering, while the next is small."

Krishna replied, "They seem so diverse, yet stand so united!

"These contrasts blend into a family that loves each other.

"What balances an indulgent father better than a disciplined mother?"

Next as they crossed the fields, Krishna exclaimed, "Radha, see these animals! Look how unique each one is.

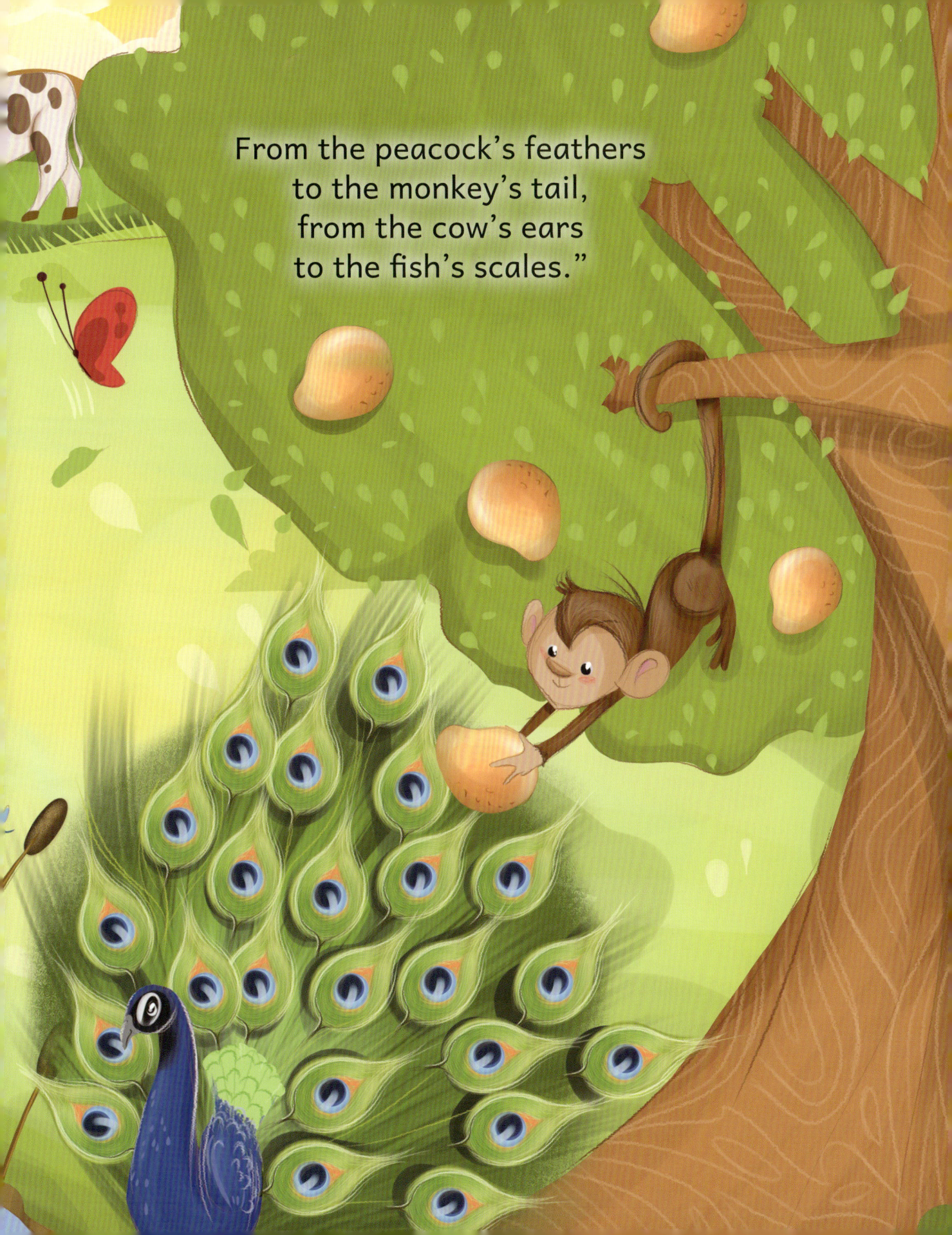

From the peacock's feathers to the monkey's tail, from the cow's ears to the fish's scales."

Farther down the road they came across
a crowd of people.

Radha shouted joyfully,
"It's Holi! My favorite time of the year!
Krishna, look at everyone in different hues.
Some in pink, some in yellow, and some in blue!"

"Yes!" Krishna agreed.
"What would the world be like
all dressed up in one color?
Holi's kaleidoscope of tones
keeps our world from getting duller!"

As they walked home together, Krishna said,
"Radha, you're right!
You and I are different,
but it's always fun around you."

"It's okay to be different," Radha continued,
"because there is no one like you.
From fighting over a fruit
to dancing while you play the flute!
All the games and all the stories you tell,
this I know fully well:
you're truly one of a kind,
a friend like you is hard to find!"

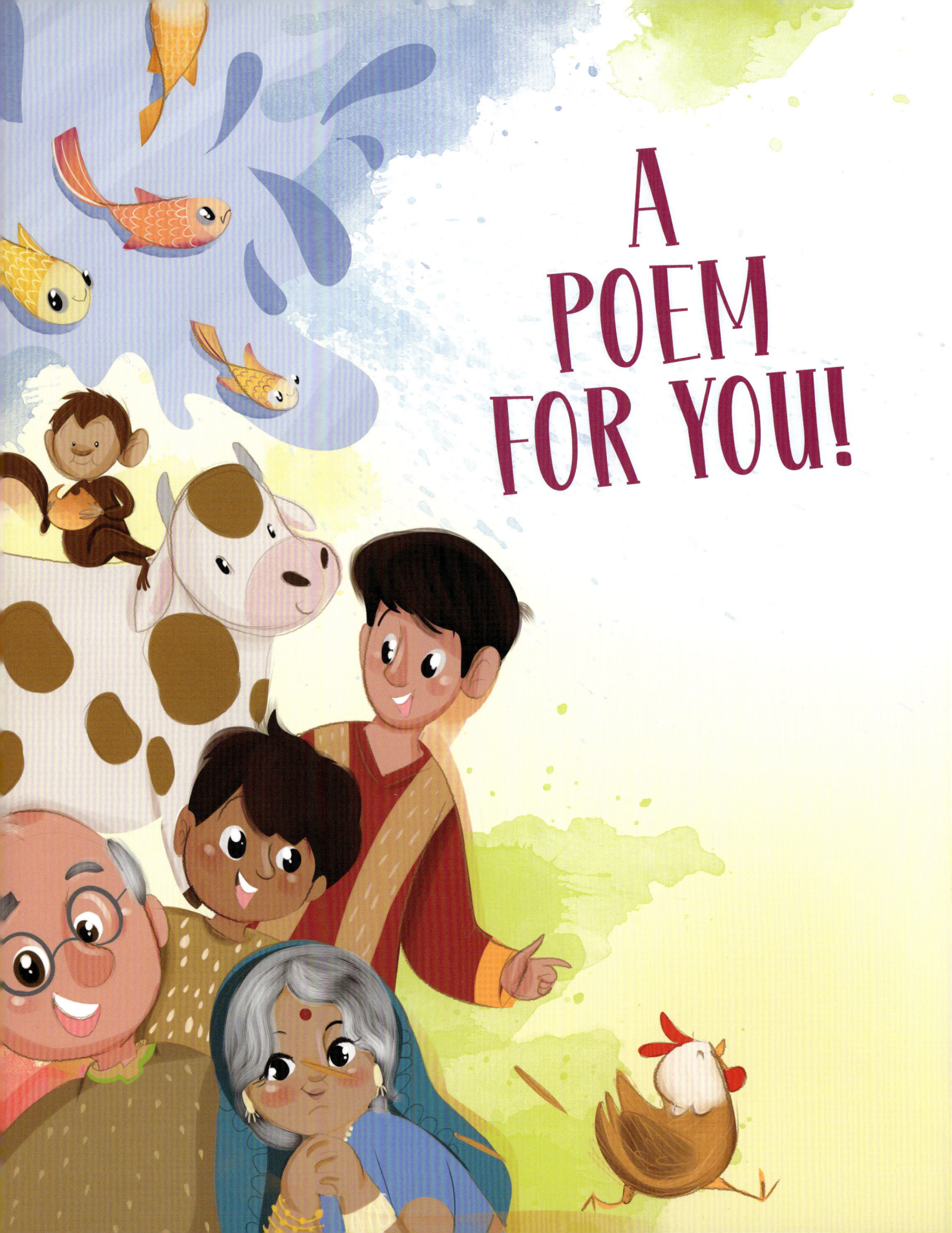

I'm me,
you're you.
I love the way I am,
you should love yourself too!

From my skin color to how I look,
my outside doesn't define me.
I'm truly one of a kind,
heart, body, and mind!

You're you, I'm me.
Together we make this world
a more beautiful place to be!

WHAT DO YOU THINK?

1. What is your favorite part of the book?
2. In what ways are **YOU** similar to others?
3. What makes **YOU** different from others?
4. How does Radha help Krishna feel better about himself?
5. What does it mean to celebrate differences?
6. Did you learn any new words from the book? What are they?

DID YOU KNOW?

KRISHNA

- Krishna is one of the most loved Hindu deities, usually shown as having dark blue skin.
- He is loving, kind, brave, and has a charismatic smile.
- He has a really sweet tooth, and he LOVES butter.
- Krishna loves playing the flute and creating beautiful melodies with it.
- Most kids in India have grown up listening to tales of Krishna's mischiefs, bravery, and benevolence.

RADHA

- Radha is Krishna's closest friend since childhood.
- She symbolizes strength and grace, supporting Krishna through good and bad times.
- It is said in Hindu mythology that Krishna and Radha are inseparable.
- In the many songs written about them, their names are always taken together.

THE FESTIVAL OF HOLI

- Holi is the celebration of colors and it also marks the beginning of spring.
- A widely popular festival, the ritual starts by lighting a bonfire the evening before, which symbolizes the victory of good over evil
- The next day, people play with various colors with their friends and families.
- Many use squirt guns to play with water, or burst water balloons! So fun!

ABOUT THE AUTHOR

When not immersed in painting a wall or conjuring ideas about her next artistic endeavor, Sonali can be found reading and understanding cultural traditions. She is inquisitive and fascinated by them, constantly finding creative ways to represent its importance in today's world. Embracing her roots, Sonali wrote her debut book as a way of bringing people together and sharing the powerful message of self-acceptance. Born and raised in India, Sonali lives in California with her husband and two teenage daughters.

◎ @author.sonalipatodia | f @Author Sonali | sonalipatodia.com